P9-DDZ-814

A Spree in Paree

by Catherine Stock

Holiday House / New York

Monsieur Monmouton had a little farm with eleven very silly sheep, five curious geese, three greedy goats, four ruminating cows, a flock of fluttering pigeons, two enormous pigs, nine noisy chickens, a rather pompous rooster, and one extremely hardworking dog.

Every morning at dawn, Monsieur Monmouton let the chickens and geese out of their pen to scratch for grubs in the farmyard. Then he milked the cows and herded the sheep and goats through the village to the pastures to graze.

Monsieur Monmouton cut and rolled up great bales of hay, weeded his vineyard, plowed his fields, and watered his vegetables. In the evening, he milked the cows again and gathered the hens' eggs. He had a very busy life.

In the summer, people from Paris camped in his field by the river. The children brought their leftover baguettes for the chickens and geese; they fed the new lambs with bottles of milk and scratched the pigs' backs with sticks. The children helped Monsieur Monmouton pick his beans and tomatoes, and they dug for potatoes and onions.

In the evening, the campers invited Monsieur Monmouton for a coffee and told him about life in Paris.

The Parisians had a wonderful time in the country.

At the end of August, the summer people loaded up their cars. "Come and visit us in Paris," they called as they drove off.

Monsieur Monmouton waved his hankie at the last car as it disappeared down the lane. "I have always wanted to visit Paris." He sighed, stretching his tired back. "I could do with a holiday. But who would look after my animals?"

When Monsieur Monmouton and his dog opened the barn early the next morning, all the animals were already squeezed into his old truck.

Beep beep! A pig pressed the horn impatiently.

"So you all want to go to Paris, do you?" Monsieur Monmouton laughed. He shrugged his shoulders, pulled his cap firmly down over his ears, and climbed behind the wheel. "*Eh bien,* let's go!"

All the way to Paris, the animals fussed about where and how they would spend their day.

SALON

When they arrived, Monsieur Monmouton circled the Arc de Triomphe and parked his truck under a shady tree on the Champs Élysées.

The sheep immediately jumped out and hurried off to the Rue de Faubourg Saint-Honoré to check out the latest fashions.

The geese waddled down to the Seine and boarded a *bateau mouche*. They sailed up and down the river and around Notre Dame, craning their necks for a glimpse of the hunchback, but all they saw were a lot of tourists.

The goats roamed around the flower beds in the Luxembourg Gardens, sniffing, and occasionally tasting, the petunias.

The cows spent the afternoon gazing at paintings of grazing cows in the Louvre Museum.

The pigeons flew to the top of the Eiffel Tower to view Paris at sunset. Everyone else had to huff and puff up the 2,710 steps.

VIN

The pigs invited their Parisian friends to a three-star restaurant and ordered the finest wines with their six-course dinner.

Finally, later that night, the chickens ushered everyone to the Follies Bergère nightclub, where they cackled and screeched outrageously at the cancan dancers, much to the chagrin of the indignant rooster. *Ooh-la-la!*

NEW YORK

The animals had a wonderful time in the city.

At daybreak, Monsieur Monmouton and his dog rounded up the animals and drove them all home.

"Never again," groaned Monsieur Monmouton as he staggered into his house and collapsed into his comfortable old armchair. "These holidays are far too much work for me."

EMPIRE STATE
IL
NY
ZATCAT
Restaura
Guide
Central Park
Staten
Islan
Ferr
the RACKETTES

But meanwhile, in the barn, the animals were already planning their next trip. . . .

For my two- and
four-legged
neighbors
in Rignac
C. S.

Printed in the United States of America
The text typeface is Soupbone.
The artwork was painted with watercolors.
www.holidayhouse.com
First Edition

1 3 5 7 9 10 8 6 4 2

Library of Congress Cataloging-in-Publication Data
Stock, Catherine.
A spree in Paree / by Catherine Stock.—1st ed.
p. cm.
Summary: Monsieur Monmouton takes
his farm animals to Paris, France,
for a holiday.
ISBN 0-8234-1720-4
[1. Domestic animals—Fiction.
2. Vacations—Fiction.
3. Paris (France)—Fiction.
4. France—Fiction.] I. Title.

PZ7.S8635 Ss 2004
[E]—dc21 2001051530